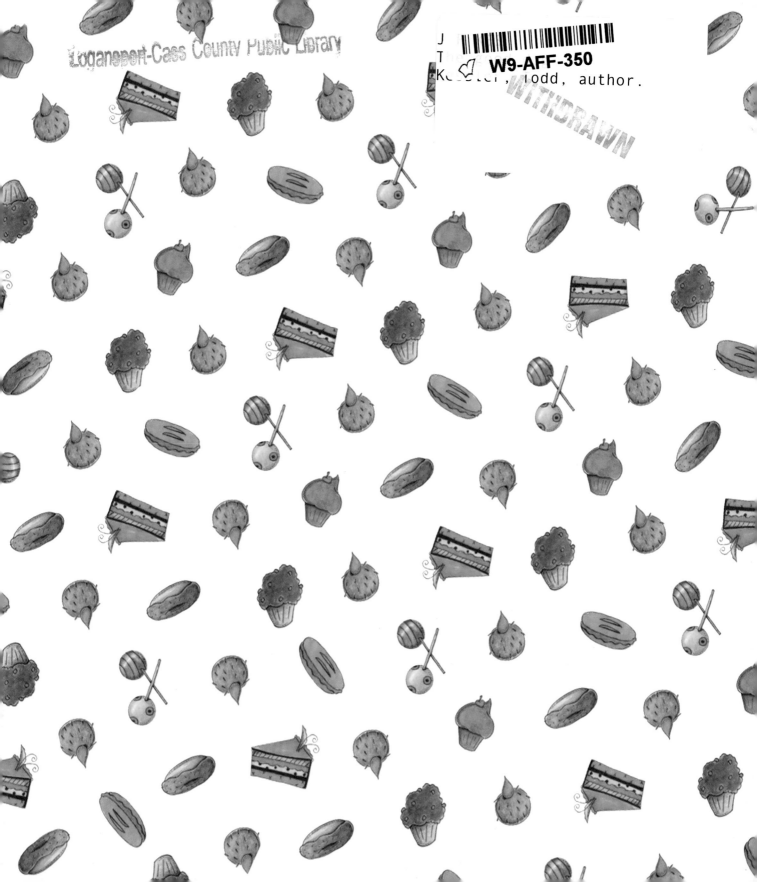

Koester, Todd, author.

The Good Dog

The Good Dog

written by **Todd Kessler**   illustrated by **Jennifer Gray Olson**

Coralstone Press

Published by Coralstone Press,
New York, NY
www.coralstonepress.com

For ordering information or special discounts for bulk purchases, please contact Coralstone Press, Inc., 235 Park Avenue South, New York, NY 10003, or info@coralstonepress.com

Illustrations by Jennifer Gray Olson
Layout by Joanne Bolton

Kessler, Todd, author.
   The good dog / written by Todd Kessler ; illustrated by Jennifer Gray Olson. -- First edition.

     pages : color illustrations ; cm

   Summary: When little Ricky Lee finds a puppy on the side of the road, he takes him home and names him Tako. Ricky is allowed to keep Tako, but only if he is a good little dog. Tako wants more than anything to be a good dog, but when greedy Mr. Pritchard hatches a plan to put the Lee family's bakery out of business, Tako may be the only one who can stop him. But to do so, he'll have to break the rules.
   Interest age level: 005-010.
   Issued also as an ebook.
   ISBN: 978-0-9898085-0-7

   1. Dogs--Behavior--Juvenile fiction. 2. Bakeries--Juvenile fiction. 3. Dogs--Habits and behavior--Fiction. 4. Bakers and bakeries--Fiction. I. Olson, Jennifer Gray, illustrator. II. Title.

[Fic]   2015909714

Printed and bound in China through Bolton Associates, Inc., San Rafael, CA 94901

10 9 8 7 6 5 4 3 2 1

For Rosa

The little puppy was curled up in a box
by the side of the road.

He was cold and afraid.

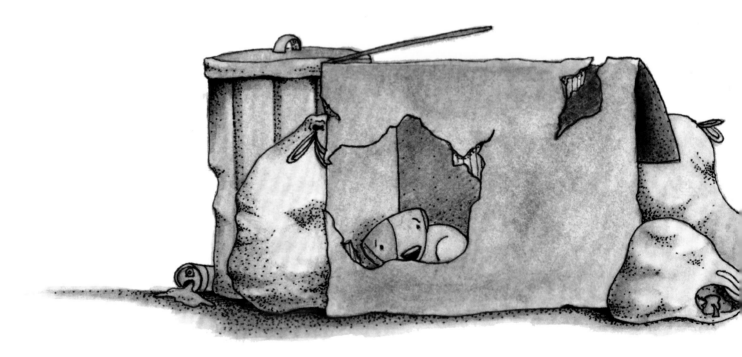

A boy on a bike came zooming down the hill ...

... and ran into the box.

"You look like you need a home," said the boy, "and I need a puppy. It's good luck that I crashed into you!"

The boy put the puppy inside his jacket and rode home.
The wind whipped in the puppy's face as he peeked out.
They were going so fast! But the puppy wasn't afraid
anymore. He felt warm and safe close to the boy.

The boy's name was Ricky Lee. His mother Mimi Lee looked sternly at the puppy. "If he's a good dog, he can stay," she said. "But if he's a bad dog, he will go to the dog pound."

"The pound is where bad dogs go when nobody wants them anymore," explained Ricky's father Papi Lee.

"He will be a good dog," Ricky promised. "I'm going to call him Tako."

Papi Lee gave Tako a piece of warm smushberry muffin right from the oven. It was the most delicious thing Tako had ever tasted.

As he munched on the muffin, Tako decided he would be a good dog, so he could stay with the Lee family forever.

But it wasn't always easy to be a good dog.

Sometimes Tako found a slipper
that needed chewing—

or honey-butter batter
that needed licking—

or a clothesline that
needed tugging.

And sometimes on rainy
days Ricky became
a monster, and Tako
needed to bark at him,

which woke the twins
Mia and Lia from their nap.

Then Mimi and Papi Lee would say, "Bad dog!"

And Tako would get very still and quiet because he did not want to be sent to the pound.

One day, the family moved to the town to open a bakery.

Papi and Mimi Lee said, "There is a lot of work to do here. Tako must be a good dog all of the time. And he must never leave the store by himself."

"Tako will be a very good dog and he will never leave the store by himself," Ricky Lee promised.

Z Z Z

Everyone worked hard to fix up the store.

Tako tried his best to be a very good dog ...

... and he never left the store by himself.

Finally the day came when Papi Lee and Ricky hung the big sign over the doorway.

At the top of the hill was another bakery called Pritchard's. It was a big store, with lots of colorless, stale sweets. People bought them anyway because, before today, Pritchard's had been the only bakery in the town.

More than anything, Mr. Pritchard loved the sound of money. He sat in his office with his little pet ferret, happily humming to the clinkety-dinkety sounds of coins dropping on the counter.

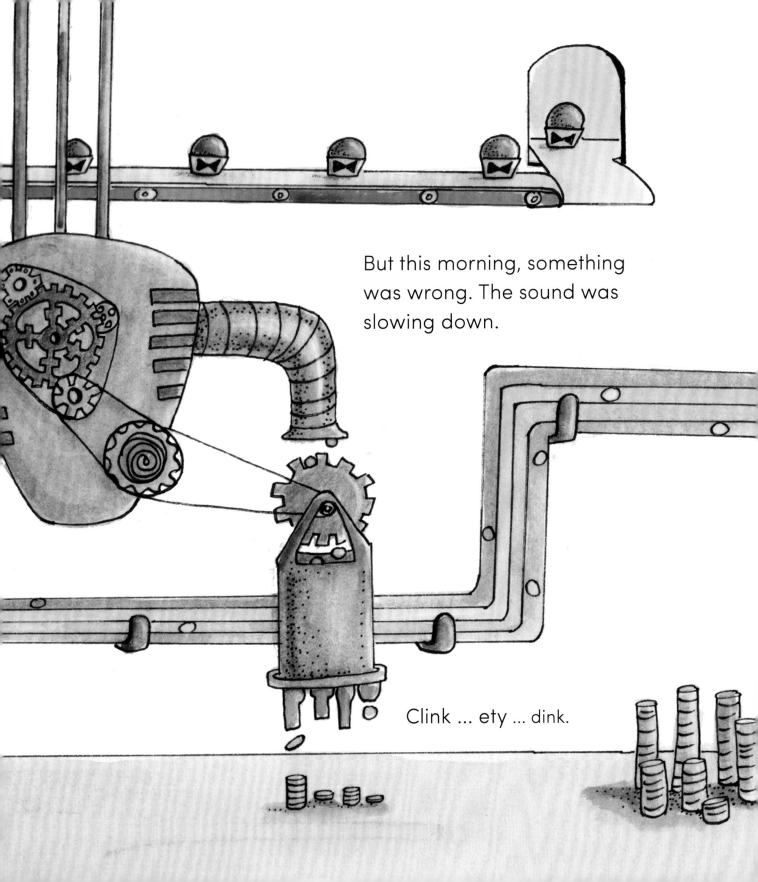

But this morning, something was wrong. The sound was slowing down.

Clink ... ety ... dink.

His store was empty! At the bottom of the hill was
a new little bakery with the most delicious sweets
he had ever seen.

There were apricot cakety-cups, snicker-doodle strudels, butterscotch bean bobs, and cherry chewbilees.

"How dare that little bakery steal my customers," Pritchard grumbled. "I can make my sweets look just as good as theirs."

Pritchard ordered his workers to make everything look fresh and pretty.

That afternoon, people saw the colorful, fresh-looking sweets in Pritchard's window. But, when they looked closely, they could see that everything was still old and stale.

"Let's keep shopping in that new Happy Family Bakery," they said. "They sell the freshest, most beautiful, most delicious sweets in this town."

Pritchard was furious. "I will ruin them," he vowed. "Then, once again, Pritchard's will be the only bakery in town!"

That night, Pritchard went behind his store and found a big flower pot. Ferret slithered inside, and then Pritchard planted the pot full of colorful flowers.

Next morning, Pritchard walked down to the Happy Family Bakery and presented Mimi and Papi Lee with the flowers. "I want to congratulate you on your beautiful new store," he said with a big smile.

"Thank you, Mister Pritchard," Mimi Lee said.

"These are very beautiful flowers," Papi Lee said. "I'll put them next to our counter."

As Pritchard walked off, Mimi Lee said, "Mister Pritchard is a very good man."

Tako liked the idea that there were good dogs, good boys, and good men.

The world was a good place.

Later that night, after the Happy Family Bakery was closed and the Lee family had gone to bed, Ferret slithered out of his hiding place and opened the door.

Pritchard snuck into the Happy Family Bakery and opened a jar containing three hundred and eighty-seven hungry beetle bugs.

When the Lees went downstairs in the morning, all that was left were crumbs ... and three hundred and eighty-seven beetle bugs, which were no longer hungry but were a lot bigger and fatter than they were the day before.

"What bad luck," said Papi Lee.

When people saw that there were no sweets left in the Happy Family Bakery, they turned around and walked up the hill to Pritchard's.

Pritchard pranced gleefully. His plan was working!

Each night, after everyone had gone to sleep, Pritchard snuck down the street and Ferret let him into the Happy Family Bakery. One night, he let loose a bowlful of slime snails.

Another night, he sprinkled weasel worms.

Each morning, the Lees wearily
cleaned up the mess.

Pritchard always stopped by on his walk. "I'm so sorry
you had bad luck again," he would say with his big smile.
"I hope your luck changes soon."

As Pritchard walked up the hill, Mimi Lee would say,
"Mister Pritchard is a good man."

"Yes, I am a good man," Pritchard said to himself. "Good and rich!"

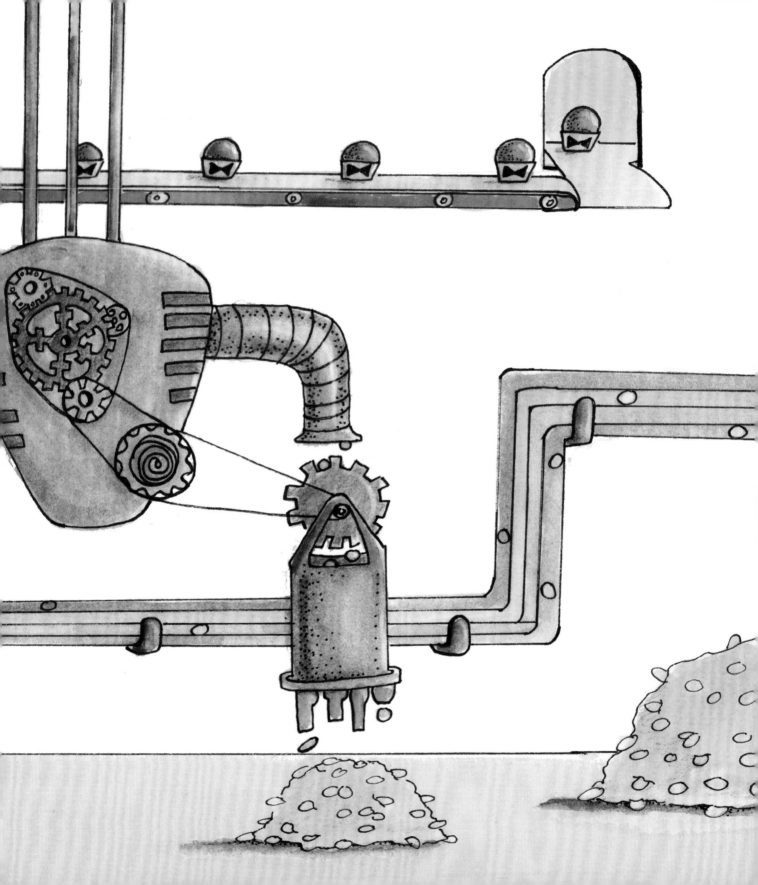

After working hard all day to clean up and bake new sweets, the Lees were so tired they slept deeply and soundly.

One night, Tako awoke— his ears pricked up— a sound downstairs.

He barked at Ricky. But Ricky was fast asleep.

So Tako went downstairs
by himself.

There were mold mice everywhere and they were eating everything in the store! Tako barked and chased the mice ...

... then he saw a man running away.

Tako chased the man up the street, barking as loud as he could. He'd make sure that bad man ran far away and would never dare to sneak into the Happy Family Bakery again!

Tako was so excited he forgot that he wasn't allowed to leave the store by himself.

The barking woke Papi and Mimi Lee. "Tako, come back now!" they shouted. "Bad dog!"

But Tako couldn't hear them because he was barking so loudly.

He chased the man up hilly streets and down narrow alleys. Finally, the man turned a corner and was gone.

Tako stopped. He had chased the man far enough, so he turned around to go home. But where was his home?

Tako was lost.

Finally, he saw something familiar—Pritchard's bakery! "Maybe Mr. Pritchard is awake," Tako thought. "He is a good man. He will help me find my way home."

Tako ran up with a happy bark.
Pritchard whipped around ...

... and then Tako saw that the back of Pritchard's bakery was crawling with slime snails, weasel worms, beetle bugs, and mold mice!

Pritchard grabbed for Tako.

But Tako leapt into the air and ran out of there as fast as he could.

"Bad dog!" Mimi Lee said. "You left the store alone."

Tako pointed his nose toward Pritchard's store and barked. But Mimi and Papi Lee were too tired to listen. "Stop barking," they said. "You will wake Ricky and the twins."

Next morning, Pritchard arrived with Mr. McCracken, the dog pound keeper. "Your dog got into my trash last night," Pritchard lied, pointing his finger at Tako. "And when I shooed him away he tried to bite me!"

Tako growled and snapped at Pritchard's finger.

"You see," grinned Pritchard, "he is a bad dog."

Mr. McCracken nodded. "That dog is going to the pound with the other dogs that are bad and nobody wants anymore."

"But I want him!" cried Ricky.

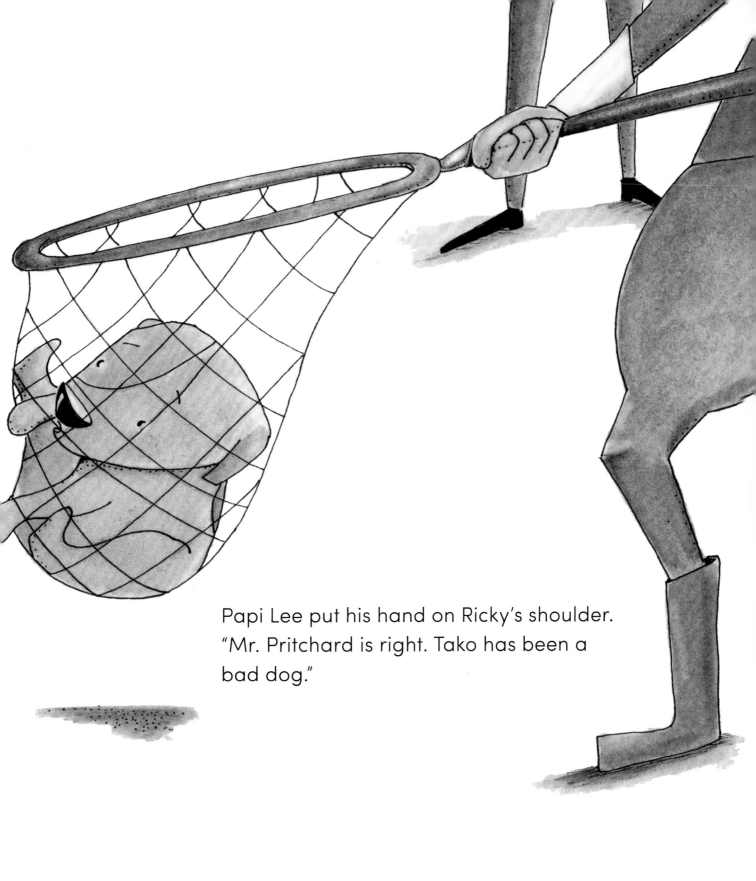

Papi Lee put his hand on Ricky's shoulder.
"Mr. Pritchard is right. Tako has been a
bad dog."

Mr. McCracken took Tako to the pound and locked him in a tiny cage.

He tossed the cage on top of other cages of bigger, unhappy, snarling dogs that nobody wanted anymore.

They growled and snapped at Tako.

It was cold in the cage. It reminded Tako of the box before Ricky found him.

Tako shivered.

Then Tako fell asleep. When Tako woke, it was late at night. He looked outside and saw Pritchard standing on top of the hill, holding a big jar.

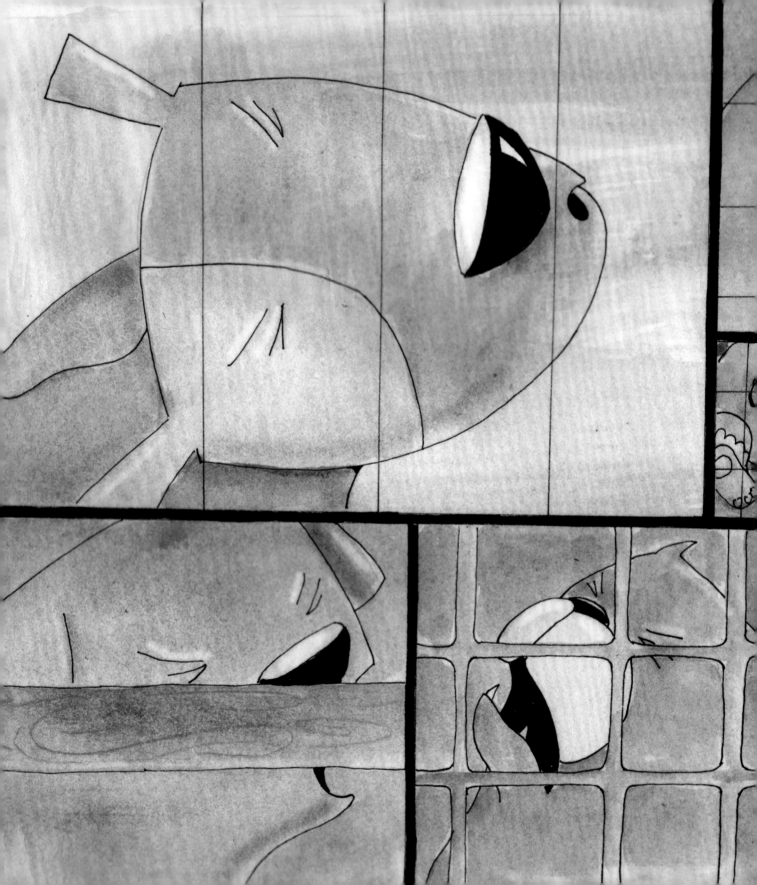

Tako howled.

The howl was so loud it rattled all the cages. The other dogs looked outside to see what Tako was howling at. When they saw Pritchard on the hill, they started howling too. Even the dogs who couldn't see out the window howled because they knew something out there needed to be howled at.

Soon all the dogs were howling and jumping up and down in their cages.

The cages shook so much that Tako's cage fell onto the floor and the door popped open!

Tako ran out as fast as he could.

Inside the Happy Family Bakery, Pritchard let out a swarm of wood wasps. The wasps whirred, eating everything that was made out of wood.

Pritchard laughed and hurried to the door, but then he saw the butterscotch bean bobs. They looked so delicious! He just had to pop one in his mouth.

And next to the bobs were the apricot cakety-cups ... the snicker-doodle strudels ... and the cherry chewbilees ... he had to try everything!

Tako ran as fast as he could. The Happy Family Bakery was falling!

Ricky shouted,
"Tako's back!
Yay!"

Papi Lee shouted, "The building is falling! Hurry!"

The Lee family scrambled outside just as the whole
building collapsed. Neighbors ran up and
stared in amazement. "Wood wasps!
How could one family have
so much bad luck?"
they wondered.

Tako saw something move in the rubble. He barked.

It was Mr. Pritchard!

Ricky Lee said, "Mr. Pritchard put the wasps in our bakery.
And he put the bugs and the snails and the worms there too.
That's why Tako growled at him!"

Mimi Lee shook her finger at Pritchard. "You wanted to have the only bakery in town. You are a bad man."

Tako growled at Pritchard.

Pritchard started running ...

... and Tako chased him out of town while everyone clapped their hands.

Pritchard kept running and running ... and was never seen again.

When Tako returned, Mimi Lee patted him on the head. "Thank you for warning us, Tako," she said. "We got out just in time! You are a good dog."

Papi Lee nodded. "Sometimes you have to be a little bit bad to be very good," he said.

That day, the neighbors began helping the Lee family build a new bakery with a cozy apartment upstairs.

When Mr. McCracken arrived, the neighbors said, "You told us Tako was a bad dog. But he was really the best dog ever. Now we all want bad dogs too!"

Mr. McCracken unlocked all the cages, and the neighbors took every single dog home.

Soon the new Happy Family Bakery was finished. The Lees had a party with free sweets for everyone.

Papi Lee gave Tako three big smushberry muffins of his own.

"You will stay with us forever," Ricky said, hugging Tako. And Tako felt safe and warm, just like he did that first day inside Ricky's jacket.

THE END

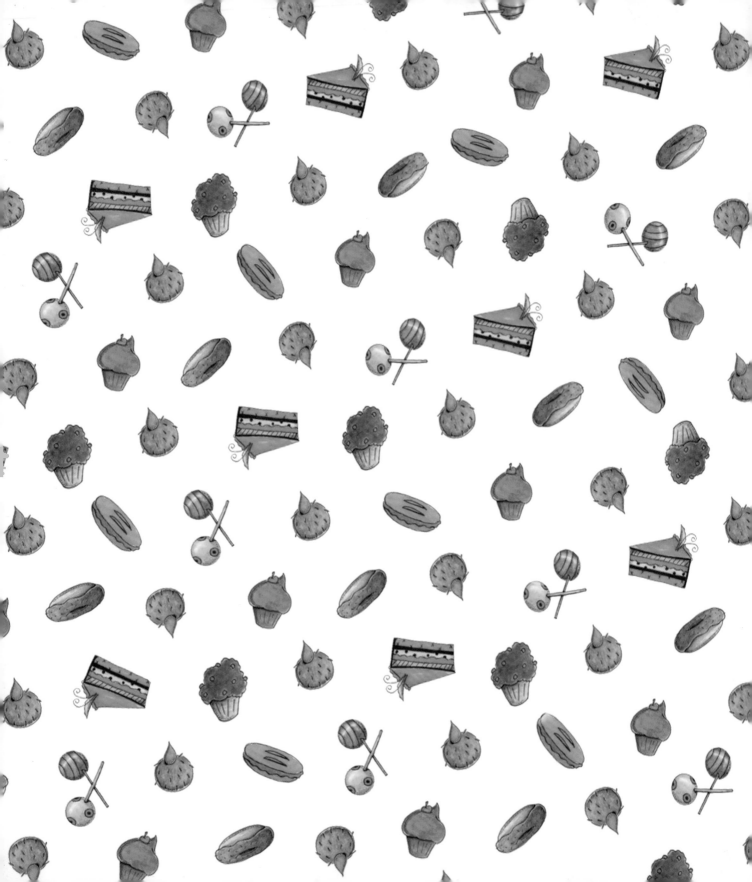